The Nana and Me Series

The Backyard Explorer

Written by Wynette Mills
Inspired by Jared Mc Ley
Illustrated by Kevan Mills

Wynette Mills

AuthorHouse™
1663 Liberty Drive
Bloomington, IN 47403
www.authorhouse.com
Phone: 1-800-839-8640

First published by AuthorHouse 8/17/2010

ISBN: 978-1-4520-2483-7 (sc)

Library of Congress Control Number: 2010911892

Printed in the United States of America

This book is printed on acid-free paper.

authorHOUSE®

Summer In The Country

Summer days with my Nana and Papa are fun.

In the backyard I see butterflies and squirrels enjoying the sun.

I like helping my Nana make Corny Corn muffins, and reading books too.

When my brother naps in the afternoon,

we write these poems for me and for you.

The Hummingbird

Hummingbird, Hummingbird how quickly you fly!

I watch for you each morning to appear in the sky.

and red food coloring

galore!

Do you see us smiling by the back door?

You float in the air like you don't have a care.

My Nana and I will always be there.

Four Little Kittens

My Nana has four kittens.

Sadly one day they ran away! Where can they be?

Are they hiding in the oak tree?

Are they chasing a bird or butterfly,
flying so gracefully in the sky?

Maybe they are chasing a field mouse around the house!

Could they be hiding under the deck?

Or watching a woodpecker peck?

Trees

Trees, Oh trees you are so good to me!

You are a friend of mine.

I wish I could climb to your very top and gaze at God's creatures below.

I might see cows and ducks and maybe a doe, and watch the river flow.
Dear Lord we love you so!

About the Author

Wynette Mills lives in a small town in the Midwest and is retired. Born and raised on a farm in Iowa, Wynette has always enjoyed the outdoors and writing. She has four children and four grandchildren. Wynette believes that spending time with her grandchildren keeps her young at heart. Grandchildren are such a blessing and we can all learn from their innocence, honesty and unconditional love. To be involved in their care is a gift and a pleasure.

This book was inspired by the summer days spent with her oldest grandson Jared when he was seven. On the first day of summer vacation he arrived at the door with his fishing hat upon his head, binoculars around his neck and writing pad in hand. With bright eyes and excitement he informed "Nana" "we are going to do some bird watching and write stories together," and so their story begins.

About the Artist

Kevan Mills lives in southern California with his wife and their ever-growing family of pets where he works as a children's book illustrator. Kevan has been a professional artist for over a decade, but his love of art began at an early age. He hasn't looked back since. Kevan earned his BFA from The Art Institute of Boston in Boston MA and continued his education in San Diego California where he worked as a video game designer.

9 781452 024837